Allie, Raj and The Difficult Monster

Written by Samreen Shah   Illustrated by Harriet Muller

For Anaiya, S.S.

For Juliet, H.M.

First published 2020 by Spencer Cavendish Books

Text © 2020 Samreen Shah, Illustrations © 2020 Harriet Muller

ISBN 9798561768637

Grateful acknowledgement is made to Dr. Reena Manghnani

I am Allie and here is a little bit about me.

I love my dog Harry, cartoons, chocolate ice cream…

And… my best friend Raj.

This is me and Raj. We've been friends since we were three. On our first day of nursery, Raj came into school dressed as Batman. He looked cool and we built CASTLES in the sand.

Sometimes Raj comes to my house after school. Raj and I play soldiers or space man ATTACKS or jungle adventure. It's all so cool. This is why Raj is my best friend. He's so much fun!

Once we built a tunnel out of blankets and chairs. We spent hours making it like a real space station. I used my dad's torch and every time we saw a space monster, I would shine my light so BRIGHT at it.

POW

Then Raj would catch the monster and trap it in the space station.

SLAM

It was hard work so mummy gave us chocolate ice cream to eat in our special creation.

YUM

Raj pretended to float and eat his ice cream at the same time. He bumped into me and the blankets fell on our heads. We laughed so much my daddy came into the room and whispered 'ssshhhh'. This made us laugh some more.

When we grow up we're going to build our own space rocket. I'm going to be the pilot and Raj is going to direct us to Jupiter.

He's already started to draw a map.

Then suddenly things were different.

This week something unexpected happened…

Raj looked sad.

On Friday, at lunchtime I asked, 'What's wrong, Raj? Do you want to come to my house and play?'

'Not really,' he said and shook his head from side to side.

'You're not being the same,' I cried and ran quickly away.

After lunch Raj sat under the table. Mrs. Applepot called his mummy and Raj went home.

While I was playing in my room, I heard mummy talking to Raj's mummy on the phone.

She said, 'Poor Raj - he feels he's caught in the middle. It must be difficult.'

I thought about this and thought some more.

Raj must have been caught by something called **DIFFICULT**.

At night I had a dream. We were in our space rocket going to Jupiter and a fire-breathing dragon came into the rocket, pulled Raj out and took him away.

Difficult is scary.

The next morning, I decided I was going to save Raj from this difficult monster.

In my rucksack I packed our monster-catching box and torch.

Hunting through wild jungles I began searching for Raj.

I looked under great rocks and on top of tall trees.

I couldn't believe what I **SAW**.

I discovered a cave and shone my torch into the dark space. To my surprise a big bear was resting inside.

'Mr. Bear,' I whispered. 'Have you seen my friend Raj? I believe he's been taken by a fire-breathing dragon.'

'Oh no,' yawned Bear, 'no one ever comes in here, but will you have tea with me? I'd rather like some company.'

I trekked for miles and miles. I saw wandering elephants and slithering snakes. Beside a huge lake there was a small snail **AWAKE**. I saw a moose on the loose and a goose drinking juice. I almost saw double when I spotted a llama blowing bubbles.

This is a funny jungle, I thought, and waved to a small monkey swinging from the trees.

'Monkey, have you seen my best friend? Was he here today?'

'No, not here, but why don't you ask Great Hunter? She lives in a yellow house on top of a green hill. She's the cleverest a human can be.'

'Thanks, Monkey.' I left him to chatter to dancing bees.

I climbed over fallen branches and swam through lakes until I spotted a bright house behind a tall gate.

I boldly knocked on the door: 'Rat-a-tat-tat.'

Great Hunter appeared. 'Can I help you?' She boomed.

'My name's Allie. I'm looking for my friend Raj who's been caught by a difficult monster.'

'Come in, young Allie,' smiled Great Hunter. 'You must be tired after walking through the jungle. Would you like to share some chocolate ice cream with me?'

I told Great Hunter about my dream. I explained I had come to rescue Raj.

Great Hunter, so very wise, said 'Raj hasn't been taken by a fire-breathing dragon. It's just that sometimes children can be sad or confused, the same as adults can be too.'

'How can I make him better? Is there a magic potion?'

'No potion my dear, but Raj will need his family to work together to help him. That's a different sort of magic.' Great Hunter said.

'I still don't understand,' I sighed.

'Well, our mind can be a bit like a room. When it's tidy you can see everything but when it's messy, everything gets mixed up and working together helps put it all back into place. Instead of books and toys these things can be our emotions and feelings. Raj may need lots of people to work together to tidy his room.'

'I prefer it when I get help to tidy my room!' I exclaimed.

'Great Hunter?'

'Yes?'

'You look like my mummy.'

Great Hunter shrugged and
gave me a warm hug.

I really did learn a lot on my great adventure. I'm very **HAPPY**. Raj will be back at school soon. I'm going to take him on a jungle walk or two. If he needs some time to himself, that's okay. Because he's my best friend who can draw the best map too!

How to use this book

This book can be used to explore feelings and introduce the idea of 'difficult' moments with your child. After reading the book, you can ask them some of these questions:

1. Why do you think Raj was sad?

2. Why do you think Allie felt cross with Raj?

3. What emotions do you think Raj was feeling when he was sitting under the table?

4. What do you think would help him feel better?

5. Have you ever found anything difficult?

6. Can you name some of the emotions you felt?

7. Talk with your child about some of the ways of managing sadness, anger or confusion. For example, they may draw a picture, talk to an adult, write a story to express their feelings.

   8. How do you think Raj and Allie felt by the end of the story?